My Mutant Stepbrothers

by Judy Baer

illustrated by Estella Hickman

*For the students and teachers
at Cando Public School.*

Published by Willowisp Press, Inc.
401 E. Wilson Bridge Road, Worthington, Ohio 43085

Printed in the United States of America

10 9 8 7 6 5 4 3 2 1

ISBN 0-87406-496-1

One

WHAT a mess! I dropped my books on the kitchen table and looked around at what used to be a neat kitchen. On my way to the fridge I tripped over some smelly, old gym shoes. I kicked one shoe so hard it landed in the sink. The whole floor was cluttered with junk like tools and weights.

Usually when I came home from school the kitchen was clean and Mom would fix me a snack. Sometimes we'd sit at the kitchen table and just talk. Then Wendy would burst in whining that her hair was a mess or that she had nothing to wear or that this absolutely gorgeous guy didn't ask her out.

Wendy's my older sister. Mostly she's a pain. But sometimes she's fun, like when she and

Mom and I go shopping at the mall and stop for pizza afterward. And sometimes, when I feel scrawny and short and my brown hair is a kinky mess, Wendy fixes my hair and lends me one of her T-shirts. At those times having a sister isn't so bad. But lately everything's changing.

The trouble started when Mom and Jake got back from their honeymoon. Jake's this big, hairy guy who used to be my mom's boyfriend. Now he's my stepdad. Why can't my mom see that he doesn't belong in our house—and neither do his two stupid sons?

Anyway, ever since Jake began moving all their stuff into our house, it's always a mess. Mom says it will get better once everyone is "settled in." She just doesn't understand. Not only have I lost my mom and my privacy—now I've lost my bedroom, too!

I guess I must have looked pretty upset because when Mom came into the kitchen, her smile sort of faded.

"Feeling blue, Darcy?" Mom asked.

"It's just that I don't see why I'm the one who has to give up my room," I snapped back.

"Jake's boys will need the space, Darcy. They'll have to sleep in your room. You can't expect your new brothers to spend the rest of their lives sleeping on the living room floor," Mom said. She tried to make a joke of it, but I could tell by the expression on her face that it was no laughing matter. "After all, you and your sister used to share a room. There was a time when you hated to sleep alone."

Yeah, I wanted to tell her. But that was when I was just a little kid. Now that I'm ten, the last thing I want to do is move into my older sister's room—especially Wendy's. It seems like Wendy is mean all the time now. Mom says it's a stage called "puberty." All I know is that it makes Wendy grumpy and stingy with her things. The other day I was looking for a book in her room and when she found me in there she nearly had a heart attack. I'm not sure what she would have done if I'd actually touched something.

"I can't see why you're being so difficult about this, Darcy," Mom sighed as she started to fix dinner. "I'm sure Wendy will be happy to share her room with you."

"Mom, what are you talking about? Wendy doesn't even want me to visit her room."

"That's not true, Darcy," Mom protested. "Be patient. Your sister's just having a hard time right now."

I thought about that for a minute. Maybe Mom was right. After Mom and Dad got divorced, Mom said we couldn't afford our big, old house anymore. And ever since we moved out of our big house and into this little one, Wendy seemed different. And she sure didn't like me anymore.

"Wendy hates me. She told me so," I insisted, even though I realized it was useless.

"Now, Darcy, you know that's not true. I know this is hard for both of you, but you've got to make the best of it."

Mom just didn't understand. With Mom's new marriage and two new stepbrothers, it could only get worse. Wendy won't have enough nerve to yell at our stepbrothers, so she'll have to yell at me.

I gave Mom a doubtful glance, but she looked so happy. She seemed so excited that this whole group of strangers was going to be a family. How could she be so thrilled when I felt like an alien in my very own home?

"Wendy says I have to sleep under the bed," I announced gloomily. "And I think she means it."

"We discussed buying a trundle bed, that's all." Mom smiled. "The mattress is only under the bed when you aren't in it. At night you pull it out to sleep on it."

Terrific. My entire room would be under Wendy's bed. She probably hadn't vacuumed under there in at least a zillion years.

"But what about my bed?"

"Eric and Ryan have to sleep on something, Darcy," Mom said.

"But that's *my* bed," I protested. When I moved out of Wendy's room and into the extra bedroom in our other house, I'd gotten a huge bed. It was perfect for a wiggly sleeper like me. Sometimes I woke up with my head where my feet should be or I would be sprawled sideways with my feet dangling over the edge. It didn't matter in that big bed.

I guess I didn't always sleep like that. After my parents divorced and my dad moved to California, I started to get kind of restless at night. I kept hearing all these creepy noises that I'd never heard before. I used to imagine rats crawling around in the attic. Sometimes I'd hear noises downstairs and think there was a burglar in the house. I'd never noticed the creaks and groans of the house when Dad was still living with us. It wasn't the house that had changed, it was us.

I guess I should get used to sleepless nights

again, now that I have to sleep under Wendy's bed. Maybe I could go live with Dad. No, that wouldn't work. Dad's hardly ever home and I'd have to leave all my friends. At least I'll be able to see him when Wendy and I visit him in California during our summer vacation. So I guess I'm stuck sleeping under Wendy for now. But I started to wonder where I would put all the rest of my stuff, like my clothes.

I asked Mom in a shaky voice, "What about my clothes?" I didn't want to cry. I tried to swallow the big lump in my throat.

"Don't worry, Darcy," Mom began. I knew immediately that she was in one of her "let's solve this problem" moods. "Remember that beautiful chest of drawers I have in my room? The one I hand-painted with roses and trimmed with lace?"

Mom loved that chest. She'd decorated it in a class she'd taken. She likes decorating things and sewing, but she hadn't had much time for that since she started working as a

9

part-time receptionist for the dentist down the street.

I nodded dumbly. How could I forget that chest? The bottoms of the drawers were made of fiberboard and some mice had gotten into it while it had been stored in the garage during our move. They'd chewed out the bottom drawer. I'm terrified of any sort of creepy-crawly thing—but mice, lizards, and snakes are the worst.

"That chest can be yours. I've always wanted Wendy or you to have it. There's plenty of room in it for all your things." Then she gave me a big hug. "Everything is going to work out. We're going to be very happy. Just you wait and see."

I wasn't in the mood to hang around and wait for this big change to happen, so I left the kitchen, slamming the screen door, and walked next door. It just wasn't fair. I'd lost my dad, my room—everything. Because of Jake and his boys, there was no place for me in the

house. I wished I could make them all go away so things could be like they used to be.

The only good thing about living in our house was that now we lived right next door to Emily Miller, my best friend in the entire world. I loved being able to walk over to see Emily anytime I felt like it.

Emily was in her backyard brushing her dog, Asparagus. She called him Gus, for short. Emily gave him that name because Gus loves to eat the asparagus plants that grow in their garden.

"Hi. What's wrong with you?" Emily asked. She could always tell how I felt by the look on my face—that's how well she knows me.

"I have to give up my room and start sleeping in Wendy's room," I muttered.

"How come?"

"Because Jake's boys are moving in."

"So Wendy's room is your only choice?"

I stared over at our little, white house. It just wasn't that big—certainly not big enough for six of us. "Some choice, huh?"

"When are they coming?" Emily asked.

"Tomorrow. They stayed with their mom while Jake and Mom were on their honeymoon." I was just beginning to learn how complicated it could be to be a kid with divorced parents. It was hard to believe that I had stepbrothers, too.

"Do you like them?" Emily asked as she finished brushing Gus's silky coat.

I thought about Eric and Ryan. Then I thought about Jake. Mom had only been divorced for six months when she and Jake started going out. I didn't think it was any big deal. I sure never thought I'd end up with a stepdad and stepbrothers.

"Well?" Emily asked impatiently.

"What?"

"Do you like them?"

"They're okay for boys, I guess. They're big. Lots bigger than me."

"Everybody is bigger than you, Sprout,"

Emily pointed out. It was true, too. I was what my mother called "petite." That meant short and skinny.

"It's going to be weird having boys wandering around your house." Emily gave a shudder. "I'm glad it's not me."

"Yeah." I flopped down on the grass next to Gus and began scratching him behind the ear. "I can't get used to having Jake around and he's been living with us for almost a week."

"What's he like?" Emily asked. Her brown eyes were wide and interested. That's her main fault—too much curiosity.

"Jake?" I paused. That was a tough question to answer. I guess I don't want to know very much about my new stepdad. Instead, I've spent most of my time avoiding him, hoping that my real dad and mom would get back together. "He's a carpenter," I finally offered.

"Really? What does he build? Houses?"

"No. Nothing like that. Smaller things. Kitchen cabinets and furniture. He works in a furniture factory. He made me a plant stand."

"Oh." Emily sounded disappointed. I suppose someone who builds plant stands isn't interesting enough for her.

I stood up. "I've got to go."

Emily looked at me carefully. "Are you going to cry?" she asked.

"Sometimes I wish I could," I said, "but it wouldn't do any good. My dad would still live on the other side of the world and Mom would still be married to Jake."

"Is it really that bad?"

"What do you think? My sister hates me and two clunky boys are going to move into my house and take over." I kicked at a clump of grass. "Then I'll be little sister to three bullies instead of just one. And," I added, "the worst part is that I don't have anywhere to hide out, not even in my own house."

Emily looked sad, but I knew she really couldn't understand what was happening to me. *She'd* never been without a place to live.

Two

AS I left Emily's house after school the next day, two fat delivery men were wrestling a trundle bed out of the back of a red-and-white truck with "Sleepytime Furnishings" painted on its side.

"Hey! Kid! Can you get that screen door?" one of them yelled.

I thought about pretending that I hadn't heard, hoping that maybe they'd give up and take the bed back to the store, but just then my mom came bursting through the door.

"Look, Darcy! Your new bed is here. Isn't it great? Wendy will have to rearrange her room. Maybe you could hang up a few of your posters . . ."

Yeah, right. Where was I supposed to hang

16

my posters—on the underside of Wendy's mattress? The whole mess seemed hopeless. I would have to share my very own space with dust, cobwebs, and unmatched dirty socks. *Thanks a lot, Mom!* I wanted to scream.

I followed the delivery men up the stairs to the bedroom. Wendy was standing by the door to her room. I could tell by the way she scrunched her mouth and crossed her arms that this wasn't going to be easy. The men had barely set the bed down when she handed me *The List.*

"Here, read this. Now. Before you touch anything in my room."

The List was two pages long and hand-written on yellow note paper.

"I didn't know you could write!" I said, just to bug her.

She was bugged all right. Her face turned pink and she glared at me. "Children!" she said, "I never plan to have any!"

I started to read Wendy's fat scrawl, but it

wasn't easy. She was into dotting the i's with little circles so the whole page looked as though it had freckles.

As far as I could tell, the only thing I *could* do in this room was tiptoe in, quietly pull out the trundle, crawl into bed, and sleep. I suppose I should be grateful she forgot "Do not breathe" on *The List*. At least I could drive her crazy making gross snorting sounds.

I wanted to tell her that it wasn't Wendy's room anymore, that it was our room. But I knew she'd ignore me.

"Here's your chest of drawers, Darcy," Mom said, dragging it into the room. "Isn't it cute?" She had it tipped so I could see the hole where the mice had gnawed at the fiberboard.

Just thinking about the mice and their disgusting claws and teeth gave me the chills. No matter how many times I told myself it was crazy, I could still imagine the whole bottom drawer full of little gray mice with tails that went on forever. I knew Mom was trying to be

nice, but even if she got down on her hands and knees and begged me, I wouldn't use those drawers.

"I'll have Jake fill in the hole on the bottom drawer. It'll be good as new then," Mom said. Who did she think she was kidding?

Just then the telephone rang and Wendy flew to answer it yelling, "It's for me!" I'm surprised her ear isn't the shape of a telephone receiver. When she said, "Hi, Gretchen," I knew Wendy would be busy talking for at least half an hour.

Mom patted the top of the dresser. "I'll let you start putting your things away, Honey. I hope you enjoy this. Eric and Ryan will be glad to have a place to put their clothes once you've moved out of your old room. Have fun."

Suddenly, she leaned over and gave me a hug. "Things will work out, Darcy. You'll see. I'm very proud of how you're adjusting to our new living arrangement. I know it's hard, but we'll soon learn to be a big, happy family."

I thought about running after her when she left the room and making her come back and open those drawers to make sure the mice were really gone, but that seemed too babyish. Instead, I dragged my blue-and-gold suitcase out of the closet and carried it to my old room.

Why did I have to leave my room? Why couldn't Eric and Ryan sleep in the garage, or better yet, in another universe?

Slowly, I began taking my clothes out of the dresser and piling them into my suitcase. It's a good thing I don't have too many clothes. Everything fit in the suitcase except for my best dresses, and I really don't care if the mice eat them. I'd much rather wear jeans anyway.

With my suitcase in one hand and my goldfish bowl tucked under my other arm, I hauled my life's belongings down the hall to Wendy's room. Even my goldfish, Finnicula, had a home. As I watched Finnicula slosh around in her bowl, I thought about something Mrs. Appletree had told us in history class. She said that there are tribes of people that have no place to live. They're called "nomads" and they just wander around the countryside.

As I carried my suitcase into Wendy's bedroom, I realized that that's exactly what I'd become—a nomad, a person with no place to sleep (unless you count sleeping under your sister's bed). Maybe I'd be better off if I were a nomad. At least nomads have their camels to sleep with. I'd rather sleep with a smelly, old camel than Wendy any day.

After I unpacked most of my stuff, I went over to Emily's. I just didn't feel like hanging around my house anymore.

Emily was just getting ready to take Gus for a walk. I liked going on walks with Emily and Gus.

We fell into a kind of rhythm as we walked. Gus was always ahead of us. Because he had short legs and a long body, he looked pretty funny when he trotted along. His back legs didn't seem to work with his front legs. Lots of times the back of his body would sway out to one side like a loose ladder on a fire engine.

"Let's take Gus past Mr. Musick's house," Emily said with this stupid grin on her face. Mr. Musick was this crabby old guy who had about a million cats.

"But won't Gus scare his cats?" I asked.

"That's the idea," Emily said.

When we got to Mr. Musick's, Emily pretended to drop Gus's leash. Gus went wild running around chasing Mr. Musick's cats, his little back legs struggling to keep up with his front legs.

Mr. Musick came out on the front porch and started yelling at the top of his lungs. Emily grabbed Gus's leash and dragged him back onto the sidewalk. Then we ran all the way back to Emily's house, stopping once to catch our breath, holding our stomachs because we were laughing so hard.

* * * * *

After supper I went to the bedroom to do my homework. Wendy was primping in front of the mirror. She puckered her lips and put lip gloss on them.

"Planning to kiss someone?" I asked.

"What would you know about it?" she snapped back.

"As much as you. Nobody would kiss you."

"Not yet, but soon." She looked rather pleased with herself and puckered her lips again. I thought she looked like a fish. Actually, Finnicula was prettier.

Wendy likes to experiment with Mom's makeup. She paints blue lines all over her eyes and makes herself look like the creature from the Black Lagoon.

She had her tape player on so loud that Finnicula was vibrating in her tank. Even a fish suffers when she has to live with Wendy.

By 8:30, I was fed up. Wendy had played the same songs a dozen times, used up all the tissues in the box, and littered junk all over the room. If I'd done that, she'd have had a fit. Instead of watching the mess get bigger, I decided to go to bed.

I pulled on the little handle at the bottom of the bed just like Mom and Jake had shown me. The mattress came gliding out and popped up into place. It was kind of funny watching my bed spring like a super ball. But when I realized Wendy the Weirdo was glaring at me, the grin fell from my face.

"What're you doing?" she barked.

"Going to bed. What does it look like?"

"You can't pull that thing out yet! It's in my way."

"Then I'll sleep in your bed. You can pull this out whenever you're ready."

"Are you kidding? This was my room first! I don't have to sleep on that thing."

Fortunately, Mom and Jake came up the

stairs at just that minute and peered into the room. I was glad to see them—until I noticed that they were holding hands. How disgusting!

"Oh, good, Darcy, you're going to bed. Wendy, why don't you turn off the light so your sister can sleep?"

Wendy gave me a look that could wilt lettuce, but she did turn off the light before she stomped out of the room.

Once I was alone and the room was quiet, I bounced a little on the bed, just for a test. It was soft enough, and it smelled brand new. But it felt weird sleeping so close to the floor. I lay down and looked up at the ceiling. It seemed farther away than it did in my old bed. I squirmed around but couldn't find any familiar little sag in the mattress to curl into. Eric and Ryan had the bed with the little sag now. I grinned into the darkness. There was only one sag and two bodies. I hoped they both fell in.

Three

I woke up the next morning with a jolt. There was a buzzer screaming in my ear. Maybe the house was on fire or there was a tornado or . . . maybe Wendy's alarm clock was going off.

"Turn it off!" I groaned. I opened one eye to peer at the face of the clock. "It's only 6:00."

Wendy put her bare feet on the middle of my back before standing up. "I've got to get dressed. I've got ensemble practice in the band room this morning. I can't be late."

She fluffed at her messy hair. "I need to do my bangs." That's how Wendy spent her life—doing her bangs.

I sighed and pulled the covers over my head.

"You'll be there before the janitor opens the

door if you get up now," I protested through the covers. Wendy ignored me. She had to be at school an hour earlier than me. Already I could see that this was going to be a disaster. It was no problem for Wendy, but it was a huge one for me.

Wendy turned on the overhead light and nearly blinded me, then she tuned the radio to her favorite rock station.

"How do you like my hair?" she asked as she studied herself in the mirror.

"I don't," I grumbled.

"You are so immature," she said. "I doubt you'll ever grow up."

"Not if I don't get some sleep," I pointed out.

She hummed as she picked out her clothes for school and clomped around like an elephant while she got dressed. At 6:30, I gave up. There was no use trying to sleep. I stumbled down to the kitchen to get something to eat.

"Up already, Darcy?" Mom asked when I

appeared in the kitchen rubbing my eyes. "You could have slept another hour."

"No one could sleep another hour in that room," I muttered, but Mom didn't seem to hear. She was shooting Jake silly grins across the breakfast table and he was flashing them right back at her.

I made some hot cereal in the microwave, then sat down at the table next to Mom and Jake.

Jake's left-handed and Mom is right-handed, so they were drinking coffee and holding hands at the same time. I was glad to see Mom happy. For a long time after Dad left she didn't smile at all. I just wish she and Jake would save the mushy stuff for some other time—a time when people weren't eating.

"How'd you sleep in your new bed?" Jake asked.

"Okay, I guess." I spooned hot cereal into my mouth so I wouldn't have to talk anymore. It wasn't Jake's fault, exactly, that I didn't like

him. It's just that I wanted my real dad to be sitting at the table next to me, sipping juice and teasing me about the way my hair looked when I woke up in the morning.

"Do you want some toast, Darcy?" Mom asked. "Eric and Ryan will be down soon . . ."

Mom didn't even have to finish her sentence for me to know what that meant. Jake's boys ate like human vacuum cleaners, sucking up everything in sight. Maybe I just wasn't used to teenage boys who took showers for hours and sprayed deodorant all over the bathroom and ate everything that wasn't locked away or growing mold.

"Yo! Hey, Sprout." As he went by, Eric patted me on the head with that great big hand that could cover a basketball. He skidded to a stop and shoveled a huge glob of cereal into a mixing bowl. Then he poured half a carton of milk over it and emptied the sugar bowl on top. He was slathering jam on a stack of toast when Ryan walked into the kitchen.

Ryan is fifteen and a year younger than Eric. I supposed that was why he had to settle for half as much cereal and being stuck refilling the sugar bowl. I couldn't believe how fast two boys could finish a loaf of bread, a gallon of milk, and an entire jar of preserves. They both chewed with their mouths open until Jake told them to stop it. How gross!

"If I'm late for school it's Darcy's fault!" Wendy announced as she came sailing into the room smelling like skunky perfume. "It's very distracting to have an extra person in my bedroom. I need my own space."

"But Darcy has been down here quite a while," Jake pointed out mildly. I was surprised to hear him stick up for me.

"Still, the idea of having to work around another whole person. . ." Wendy let the sentence fade away dramatically.

It sounded like she was talking about an 800-pound whale. Who was she kidding?

"You'll get used to it. Darcy didn't complain," Jake said. He was sticking up for me again. I stared at him, wondering if this was some kind of trick he was pulling to get me to like him. He gave me a warm look that said he understood how hard it was being Wendy's sister.

"Doubtful," Wendy said. Then she smiled at Jake. It was gross. Wendy was nicer to Jake than she was to her own sister! She had liked Jake ever since he and Mom started dating, so she tried not to get mad when he pointed out her faults. And believe me, she had plenty of faults!

After Wendy and the boys left for school, I went upstairs to get dressed. It was great having the room all to myself. I decided that it was pretty handy having all my clothes in my suitcase. There was no running around the room looking for things. If it wasn't in there, I didn't have it. It was that simple.

Since Wendy was gone, I figured I'd just sort of borrow some of her stuff. She'd never know. Besides, she had so many rules that I was bound to break one or two.

Just to be safe, I closed the door. Then I used Wendy's blow dryer and hairbrush to create this puffy hairstyle that I'd seen in a magazine. I looked through her closet, too, but most of her stuff was geeky-looking. I put on some jeans and a T-shirt. When I pulled the T-shirt over my head, it kind of messed up my hair. I guess it takes practice to look good.

Someone knocked on the door. I quickly put Wendy's things back in place before I forgot. I didn't want nuclear missiles going off in my direction when Wendy got home.

"It's open," I called out.

The door opened. "Need a ride, Darcy?" Jake asked as he stood in the open doorway. He looked big and cozy in faded jeans and a plaid shirt.

I was tempted to accept his offer just because he was nice to me at breakfast. I looked up into Jake's hopeful eyes and finally said, "No, I have to feed Bruno."

Bruno is my little beagle puppy who gets into everything. When he's not outside, we have to keep him in the laundry room so he doesn't chew things up. One time he ate one of Wendy's new lipsticks. Boy, was she mad!

"I can wait for you, Darcy," Jake said.

"No, thanks. I've got some other stuff to do."

"Okay. If you're sure," he said, hesitating for a moment at the door.

"I'm sure." Suddenly, I felt like I'd swallowed a brick. I realized that I'd grown weak and had almost been nice back to Jake. What would Dad say about that? He would think that I didn't love him anymore. And I never wanted that to happen—not in a zillion years.

I never wanted to forget anything about my dad. I wanted to remember the way he smiled, the way he smelled, the way he ruffled my hair. The only way I could remember every single thing about Dad was to make sure that Jake didn't get in the way. I couldn't like Jake too much. Why couldn't he just be our neighbor instead of my stepfather? Then I could've liked him as much as I wanted.

Mom walked into the room and caught Jake just as he was going out the door. He hugged Mom and gave her a good-bye kiss that made me look away. Then he tugged at my ear, like he often did, and murmured, "Bye, Darcy. Have a good day."

I nodded but didn't answer. My heart was hurting like it usually did when I thought about my dad.

After Jake left, I went downstairs, poured a bowl of puppy food, and took it to the laundry room. Bruno was waiting for me, his little tail wagging so hard it almost slapped him on his sides. When I leaned down to put his dish on the floor, he jumped up and gave me a wet, sloppy kiss.

Bruno had cried the first two nights he'd had to sleep in the laundry room, but he'd gotten used to it. Mom and Jake didn't want to take a chance on Bruno having an "accident" on the new carpeting, especially while he was a puppy.

Bruno was probably the best and worst present I'd ever gotten. Every time I looked at him, my eyes felt scratchy, like I was going to cry. I'd always wanted a puppy but I could never have one before because Dad was allergic to dogs.

When Bruno arrived last month in a big, white box with a red bow and a "Happy Birthday, Darcy" card attached, I was so happy I could hardly believe it. And when I opened the package and saw this shaggy, wet-nosed puppy, it was instant love.

But then I realized that the package from the pet shop wasn't from my dad—it was from Jake. I felt guilty loving something Jake had given me. My dad had sent me a gift certificate for the bathing suit I wanted. I didn't want to love Bruno more than my bathing suit, but you couldn't hug a bathing suit.

I watched Bruno eat for a minute, then picked up my backpack and headed out the back door. About halfway to school, I was sorry I hadn't taken Jake up on his offer. He had asked so sweetly that it had taken a lot of strength to resist. I guess he could be kind of like an uncle or something—just as long as he didn't try to take my dad's place. I wanted him to remember that I already had a dad of my own.

After school Emily and I went over to her house. Her mom had made a big batch of double-chocolate deluxe fudge. I was glad, because I wasn't in any hurry to go home. When Wendy, Eric, and Ryan all brought their friends home at once, it was too noisy and crowded. Besides, Emily has a big bedroom all to herself.

I flopped down on her bed and looked around. There were posters and bulletin boards everywhere. Emily even had little hooks to display special stuff like the silk robe her parents brought her from San Francisco's Chinatown and the crepe-paper grass skirt we'd made at camp.

"You don't know how lucky you are to have your own room!" I said. It was hard not to be jealous—especially since I felt like a ten-year-old nomad. "Wendy wants me to drop off the face of the earth."

"No, she doesn't," Emily protested. "You worry way too much. You're lucky, too. You just don't know it."

"Emily, I live out of a suitcase."

"That's because you're weird," she said calmly. "Look at all the good things you have going for you! For one thing, you have good-looking stepbrothers."

"They usually ignore me."

"And a sister..."

"...who hates me."

"And your parents..."

"My parents are divorced."

"You have a great new dad."

"He's not my dad."

"But he's nice."

"I don't like him."

"You haven't tried."

"I don't want to try."

"He gave you a puppy."

That stumped me. Jake had given me Bruno. Dad should have been the one to give me Bruno, not Jake. It made my stomach hurt to think about it.

Emily flung herself into a big, yellow bean bag chair that was piled high with stuffed animals. "What are you going to do?" she asked.

"About what?" I asked.

"About hating your stepfather and your stepbrothers."

"I never said I hated them. I just don't want to live with them," I replied.

"So what are you going to do?"

"Move out," I blurted. As soon as I said it, I knew it was the best idea I'd had in ages.

"Move out?" Emily's eyes got as big as Frisbees. "Of your house?"

Her panicked expression made me giggle.

"No, silly. I'm going to move out of the bedroom!"

It was a great idea, a stupendous idea! There was only one little problem. I didn't have anywhere else to go.

Four

I couldn't face going home alone that night so I called Mom and asked her if Emily could come over for dinner. She said it was fine and Emily's mother said it was okay as long as Emily walked Gus after dinner.

I promised Emily I'd help her walk Gus if she would come for dinner.

"Hey, you could bring Bruno along," Emily suggested.

"I don't know. He's so shy that he runs under my legs every time he hears a noise."

"Well, he'll never learn to overcome his fears if he doesn't get out in the world," Emily advised. Sometimes she sounds like Ann Landers.

"Let's go eat," I said, switching the subject.

As we left Emily's house, Gus barked good-bye to us. By the time we got to my house, everyone was waiting at the table. Eric and Ryan were already slopping mounds of food onto their plates. They really were disgusting. I wasn't sure I could sit there for a whole meal and watch them eat.

Dinner was pretty boring. The phone kept ringing and Wendy kept jumping up from her seat to answer it. I still don't know why anyone would want to call her.

"I'm glad Mom let me come for dinner," Emily announced. Eric and Ryan had been telling her jokes for half an hour and everyone was laughing—except me. "It's lots more fun here than it is at my house. My dad doesn't even know any funny jokes."

"We'd better keep her here, then," Ryan said to Eric. "We've finally found someone who appreciates our sense of humor. Have you heard the one about..."

I quit listening to the conversation. I

couldn't stand it. Emily had been here half an hour and she seemed to be loving every second of it. The boys were doing everything they could to make her laugh.

It was no wonder that Emily loved to come over and talk to Jake and the boys. They always had a new joke to tell her. She thought my new family was great.

I didn't. I wanted my dad to come home and eat dinner with Mom, Wendy, and me.

"More potatoes, Darcy? Gravy?" Jake held out the bowl, tempting me. "When I was younger, I used to make volcanoes out of my mashed potatoes. Then I'd scoop on the gravy and pretend it was lava pouring over the sides. "Do you want to try it?" he offered.

He was doing it again. He was trying to make me like him. I stared down at my dinner plate. I wished he'd quit trying to be so friendly.

"Darcy, be polite. Answer Jake," Mom said.

"No, thanks," I mumbled, even though I did want to make volcanoes out of my potatoes. I couldn't give in now. Jake was the enemy, wasn't he? If he hadn't married my mom and moved his boys into our house, I'd still have my own room—and maybe my dad, too. No, I couldn't give in now.

"May Emily and I be excused?" I asked. Eric and Ryan were still shoving food into their bottomless stomachs and making gross noises when they slurped down their milk. Wendy was dieting and making a big deal over eating a couple little hunks of roast beef and a lettuce leaf. It all made me sick.

"You guys are really funny," Emily said, laughing at the digusting sounds they were making.

"Didn't you promise your mom you'd walk Gus after dinner, Emily?" I asked.

"Oh, yeah, I almost forgot, I was having so much fun."

How could Emily be having so much fun when I was so miserable?

I got Bruno while Emily went home for Gus.

We met on the front sidewalk of my house and started walking. Bruno and Gus made a funny pair. Gus kept bumping into Bruno, then Bruno would yelp and run between my legs. We didn't get very far. I decided it would be easier to pick Bruno up and carry him.

"He's so cute," Emily said, petting Bruno.

I held Bruno closer, cuddling him tightly.

Gus barked as if to say, "What about me?"

Emily stooped down to pet Gus. "You're a good dog, too, Gus. Dogs are great," Emily said. "They always love you no matter what. Sometimes when I'm feeling sad, all I have to do is look at Gus's tail wag and it makes me happy."

"I know what you mean. When Bruno licks my nose, he makes me laugh."

Emily didn't have to say anything. I knew what she was thinking. Jake gave me Bruno to make me happy. Maybe Jake wasn't so bad, after all.

After Emily left, I put Bruno back in the laundry room and went upstairs to Wendy's room. I couldn't call it my room. She wouldn't let me hang a poster or leave my clothes on the bed. There was no use staying in a place that made me feel like a cockroach.

There had to be another place for me to stay. Even though I wasn't tired and it was too early for bed, I took my rolled-up sleeping bag and my suitcase and went into the hall. I wanted my stuff with me—just in case I found a good place to sleep.

I peeked into my former bedroom, the one Ryan and Eric had stolen away from me. There were tennis shoes and clothes everywhere. They'd piled baseball equipment on my beautiful little window seat and taken down my pink curtains. And my favorite bed in the whole world was a complete mess. Why didn't Jake yell at them to clean it up? Maybe I should sick Wendy on them.

It wasn't easy dragging both my suitcase and a sleeping bag down the hallway, but there was no way I was going back into Wendy's room. The door to Mom's room was open and I could see Jake's big boots sitting by the dressing table. Even seeing his boots where my dad's shoes used to be made me sad. Jake and his boys had taken over the entire house. Their junk was everywhere. This morning, I'd even had to step over their shoes to get out the door. Those shoes were so big they looked like I could sail down a river in them.

When I got to the bathroom, I had to stop and rest. My suitcase was heavier than I'd thought. I tipped it on its side and sat down. As I sat there, an idea began to form in my brain.

In one corner of the room was a huge bathtub. It was as long as my trundle bed but not quite as wide. My sleeping bag would fit perfectly along the bottom. Maybe if I wiggled around enough I could snuggle myself in for a good night's sleep.

"It's a crazy idea, Darcy!" I said out loud. Then I thought about it a little more. Anything was better than sleeping under Wendy's bed. Just as a test, I unrolled my sleeping bag in the bottom of the tub. A perfect fit. With a pillow and a stuffed animal or two it would be even better than the trundle.

During the day, the family used the half bath downstairs. This bathroom was only busy in the mornings when everyone wanted to take showers. If I slept in the tub, I'd have to get up early so no one ran water on me.

I wiped a few water droplets off the sides of the tub and patted my sleeping bag into place. I opened my suitcase and took out my pajamas and Frederick, my stuffed panda. It only took a minute to change and crawl into the tub.

My sleeping bag felt smooth and cool as I lay on top of it. It didn't take me very long to begin wishing that I had some kind of a mattress beneath me. The tub was hard—very hard.

The hardness of the porcelain didn't bother

me nearly as much as the little slope of the tub where my head was resting. My neck was tilted upward at an angle that made it ache. But I decided it was better than having Wendy boss me around every minute.

Suddenly, the door to the bathroom flew open and Jake walked in. I felt pretty silly lying there in the bathtub. I just stared at Jake, daring him to say anything to me. His eyebrows lifted so high that they were hidden under the brown hair that fell over his forehead but he didn't say a word. He just mouthed the words, "Good night, Darcy," turned around, and left the room. Jake really surprised me. He didn't yell or lecture or order me back into Wendy's world of rules. If my mom or my real dad had found me sleeping in the bathtub, there definitely would have been fireworks. I wondered why Jake hadn't yelled at me. He sure was hard to figure out.

Falling asleep was easy, but waking up was painful. I had a crazy dream that I was a

sardine packed in a little tiny can. And the worst part was that I was packed so tightly I couldn't twist or turn or get comfortable. When I woke up in the middle of the night, I realized that sardine cans and bathtubs are a lot alike. There's no way to get comfortable in either one of them.

My neck felt like it was broken. Not only had I lost my bedroom, I'd also put a permanent kink in my neck. I was sure I'd be walking around with my head bent to one side for the rest of my life.

As I tried to straighten my neck, I realized that something else was going wrong at the other end of my body.

My feet and the entire end of my sleeping bag were soaking wet. When I twisted and turned to get comfortable, I must have kicked on the faucet.

I pushed away my wet sleeping bag and stood up. A shiver ran down my spine. Every part of my back hurt.

"Owwww!"

Carefully, I stepped out of the bathtub. My legs weren't working very well. They were wet and rubbery. I rescued Frederick and hauled the sleeping bag over the side of the tub. I couldn't sleep in that anymore tonight.

Luckily, everyone was asleep. All the bedroom doors were closed and no one heard me grab a blanket from the linen closet. I tiptoed down the stairs and headed for the living room. The couch looked awfully inviting. Then I heard Bruno scratching on the laundry room door.

When I went in to say hello, he wagged his tail so hard his entire body shook. He looked so pitiful and lonesome.

"Can I sleep with you, Bruno?" I asked. He wagged his tail furiously, signaling a definite "yes."

I spread the blanket on the floor next to the heater. At least my feet would be dry here. Besides, I loved the sweet, clean smell of fabric softener. This might be just the place for me to sleep.

When I lay down, I realized that a tile floor wasn't much softer than a bathtub. I sat up and looked around the room. Eric and Ryan's dirty clothes were heaped in a big pile by the washing machine.

I snapped my fingers. I'd finally found a reason to be thankful for big brothers. I jumped to my feet and spread the clothes out evenly across the floor and covered them with my blanket. When I snuggled down into the mattress made of boys' clothes, I sighed. It was a hundred times softer than the bathtub. Maybe I shouldn't have been so hard on Eric and Ryan after all.

I was just drifting off to sleep when Bruno stuck his nose in my ear. Bruno must have figured that I'd come to spend the night playing with him. He picked up his rubber bone and dropped it on my chest. I could smell his hot, puppy breath as he panted in my face.

Then, when I didn't pick up the bone and give it a toss, he stuck his nose into my ear and gave a great big snuffle.

When that didn't work, he began to lick my face. With a doggy sigh, he curled up beside me and laid his head in the crook of my arm. Every few minutes Bruno stuck out his long, pink tongue and licked my cheek. It tickled but I didn't care. It felt wonderful to have his warm little body next to mine.

Just as I was dozing off, I realized that I'd left Frederick lying on top of the dryer. I smiled. He would be okay this one time. Tonight I had a real, live teddy bear to cuddle.

Five

"**Q**UIT it, Wendy! You're pulling my hair!" I yelled.

The sound of my own voice woke me from my dream. I brushed furiously at my hair for a moment before I realized that my sister wasn't pulling at my hair, she wasn't even in the room.

I blinked sleepily and took a deep breath. Then the smell of dirty clothes brought everything back to me in a rush. I remembered dragging my soggy body from the bathtub to the laundry room in the middle of the night.

Wendy couldn't be here. She refused to set foot in the laundry room. Then who was pulling my hair?

As I rolled my head to one side I heard

something crunch beneath me.

"Bruno! I'm sorry, Bruno!" I told him.

Poor Bruno. He'd probably never slept with anyone who was such a restless sleeper. Somehow I'd managed to flip-flop myself around until I'd landed with my head in his bowl of puppy food. Bruno was picking kibble out of my curls and crunching it in his sharp little teeth.

Just then Ryan opened the laundry room door. He stared at me lying there with Bruno chewing happily on my hair. Then he cupped his hands around his mouth and yelled, "Dad! Come here. You've got to see this! You won't believe it!"

I didn't even have time to chase Bruno away before Jake appeared in the doorway. He looked especially big and scary as he stood there, filling the entire door. Because I was lying on the floor, looking up at him was like trying to see the top of a mountain.

Jake's lips got all tight and weird looking,

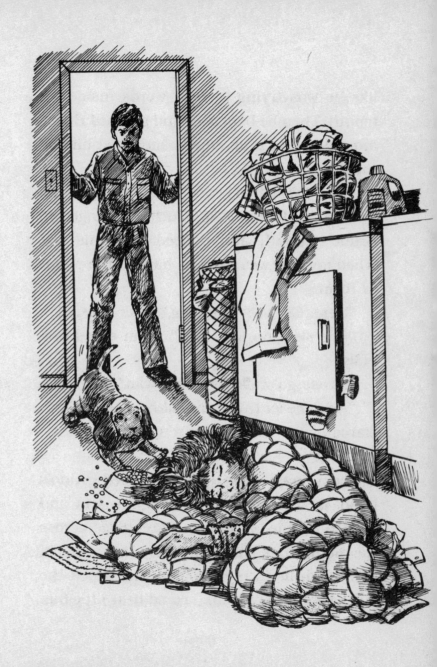

like he was trying to hold words inside his mouth. Then he bent over and grabbed Bruno around his fat little middle and lifted him off the floor.

"Ow!" I yelled, as I tried to pull my hair from Bruno's clutches. Jake stuck his finger in Bruno's mouth and popped open his jaw. When my hair was freed he handed the puppy to Ryan.

"Here. Go walk this dog," Jake ordered.

"She slept on the floor?" Ryan asked stupidly.

"Please go walk the dog, Ryan."

"And she let this mutt eat her hair?" Ryan stared at me as if I were a space alien.

"Now."

Ryan finally shut up and grabbed Bruno's leash. He tucked Bruno under his arm and headed for the back door. Jake walked across the room, stuck his hands under my armpits, and lifted me to my feet. Then he wiped the dog food out of my hair. I could hear little bits of kibble falling to the floor.

"Don't you think this has gone far enough?" Jake asked.

I felt a tightness in my chest that made me want to explode. No one but my real dad could talk to me that way. No one!

I narrowed my eyes to little slits and glared at him. "I have to get ready for school now," I said, daring him to argue with me. He wasn't my father. He had no right to tell me what to do.

He sighed and shook his head. "Go ahead. I'll sweep up the dog food before your mother sees it."

I rushed out of the laundry room without looking back. I didn't want him to see the tears rolling down my cheeks.

*　*　*　*　*

"If you're finished eating breakfast, Darcy, I'll take you to school," Jake said. "I see Emily

61

coming up the sidewalk."

"Hi!" Emily said as she walked into the kitchen.

"Need a ride?" Jake asked.

Emily nodded eagerly. She liked it when Jake took us to school. I wasn't sure if she was more excited about Jake or about the ride. Emily was basically lazy. We rode with Jake mostly because I didn't want to hear Emily complain that her feet hurt all the way to school.

In the car, Jake was kind of quiet. Ever since he'd found me in the laundry room that morning, he hadn't talked to me much. Emily didn't seem to notice. She kept talking about Gus and school and she must have thanked Jake about a million times for taking us to school.

At school, Emily was full of questions, especially after I'd told her how I'd spent the night in the bathtub and the laundry room.

"Why did Jake let you stay there?" she

asked. "I don't understand."

I didn't really understand either, so I just shrugged.

"I think you're making a big deal out of nothing," Emily said.

"What's that supposed to mean?" I asked.

"I think Jake is being pretty nice to you."

"Nice? Are you kidding?" I wrinkled my nose in disgust.

"You just don't want to like him because he's your new dad," Emily said. "Maybe you're just not used to him yet."

"Don't call him that!" I yelled. "He's not my dad and he's never going to be my dad, either." I could feel my face getting hot.

"I didn't mean to make you mad," Emily muttered. "I didn't know you'd get so upset."

"No one can take my real dad's place, Emily. I just wish Jake wouldn't even try," I said.

Emily stared at me. I didn't like the feeling. She knows me so well that sometimes I don't want to hear what she has to say.

"Can Jake be all that bad if he's making your mom happy?" she asked finally, scuffing her toe on the floor. "Every time I see her she's smiling."

"You don't understand," I told her. "You can't. Your mom and dad aren't divorced. You don't have strangers running around your house."

I had a sinking feeling in my stomach—and then I knew why. Even Emily was being charmed by Jake and the junior dweebs he calls sons. Couldn't she see what was happening? Couldn't anyone see how Jake was worming his way into our lives—that what he really wanted to do was replace my father? I had this feeling that it wouldn't be long before no one except me remembered my dad.

After school, Emily babbled on about a lot of stuff, but I didn't really pay much attention. In fact, I was in kind of a daze, like I was sleepwalking or something, until after dinner.

By the time we finished eating dinner, I

was dreading the rest of the night. I was already worrying about where I would sleep. I wouldn't go back to Wendy's room and I'd already given up on the bathtub and the laundry room. The only thing I could do was put off going to bed for as long as I could. If I stayed up late enough, maybe Mom and Jake would get tired and go to bed early. Then I could sleep cozily on the couch.

While Jake and Wendy were helping Mom clean up, I took my suitcase out of the laundry room and carried it into the living room. I hid it behind a chair. If I did get to sleep on the couch tonight, I wanted my things nearby.

"What are you doing, Sprout?" Eric asked. I nearly jumped out of my skin when I heard his voice near my ear.

"Oh...nothing," I fibbed.

"Still carrying that dumb old suitcase around, huh?" he asked.

"It's not dumb and it's not old!" That suitcase held everything I owned. Didn't the big dummy know it was because of him that I had to live out of a suitcase?

"Don't be so grouchy, Sprout," Eric said with a grin. "Come on. How about a game of gin rummy with Ryan and me?"

"My name's not Sprout."

"Okay," Eric said, bowing deeply to me and speaking in some kind of corny accent. "Darcy dear, would you be kind enough to indulge in a game of gin rummy with me and my brother, Ryan?"

I tried to hide the smile that crept on my face. Then I admitted, "I don't know how to play."

"No problem. We'll teach you."

"Really?"

"Sure. If you promise to be better at it than Wendy. We've given up on her."

"I could have told you that would happen," I said. "Wendy doesn't follow instructions unless they come in a teen magazine or on a lipstick tube."

Eric grinned his friendly, lop-sided grin and flopped his big arm around my shoulders. Ryan was already shuffling cards at the kitchen table. When we walked into the room together, both Mom and Jake smiled like we'd brought them a big present. It took me a minute to realize that they were smiling because Eric had his arm around me and I wasn't socking him in the stomach trying to get him to stop.

"Can she play better than Wendy?" Ryan asked.

"I sure hope so," Eric said. "There's no way she could be worse."

"True. Okay," Ryan said, "here are the rules..."

The time went by quickly. Eric and Ryan were great card players, and they were good teachers. Neither of them got mad at me when I made a mistake. They just kept saying that I was much better than my sister and to not worry about it. And for a little while, I almost forgave them for stealing my bedroom.

Just as I'd won my first game, Jake called out, "Boys, have you done your homework?"

"Uh-oh," Ryan muttered. "Got to run, Sprout."

Eric scooped the cards into a pile and whispered to me, "Party's over."

In a second, they were bounding up the stairs.

"They sure must've had a lot to do," I murmured.

Jake chuckled. I hadn't meant to be funny.

"What are you two giggling about?" Mom asked as she came up behind us and wrapped her arms around both of us.

While Jake filled her in, I slipped away from Mom and headed for the laundry room to check if my sleeping bag was dry. Bruno nipped at my toes, inviting me to play.

"Not tonight, Boy. I have to sneak this into the living room before Mom sees me." If I did get to sleep on the couch, I didn't want to be without my sleeping bag.

When I returned to the kitchen, Mom was turning out the lights. "We're tired tonight, Darcy," she said. "Jake and I are going to bed early. Wendy and the boys are doing their homework. Are you coming upstairs?"

"I'm going to get something to eat first," I said.

"Okay. Good night, Honey," Mom said, then she kissed the top of my head. She smelled clean and fresh—like fabric softener—only nicer. Then she hugged me tightly and gave me her "it's-going-to-be-all-right" smile. "Come upstairs when you're done, Darcy."

As soon as she was gone, I grabbed a doughnut and headed for the living room. The couch looked so wonderful—soft, cozy, and warm. I had my sleeping bag spread across it when I heard footsteps on the stairs.

I could hear Mom and Jake talking as they came down the steps. "Are you sure you want to watch this program tonight?" Jake asked.

"I thought you said you were tired."

"I am, but it's supposed to be a great movie. I almost forgot it was on tonight."

Mom and Jake had changed their minds and were coming back to watch a movie! With a quick jerk, I tossed my sleeping bag over the top of the couch and dived after it. I was barely out of sight behind the couch when I felt someone sit down.

"Isn't that Darcy's suitcase?" Mom asked.

"The one she's been dragging around the house?" Jake asked gruffly. "Looks like it."

"Poor kid. She's been so upset lately."

"I wish there'd been another place for the boys to sleep," Jake said. "I'm sorry that she had to lose her bedroom."

"She'll adjust to all this," Mom said. "Darcy's very strong."

"I don't know. I'm worried about her," Jake said softly.

I couldn't hear what Jake said next. It was weird to listen to them talking about me. Soon the movie started and I heard Jake chuckle. A minute later, Mom was laughing, too.

I looked around the little triangular-shaped space behind the couch. I was trapped. Jake and Mom definitely weren't going anywhere for at least two hours. Carefully, I arranged my sleeping bag beneath me. My cozy space was warm and dry and the carpet made a nice, soft padding. Sleeping behind the couch wasn't such a bad idea.

Every few minutes Jake and Mom chuckled. The more they laughed, the sleepier their voices made me. The low hum of the TV and the stuffy air behind the couch made my eyelids feel like they weighed a thousand pounds each. I couldn't keep them open one second longer.

*　*　*　*　*

Suddenly, my eyelids popped wide open as I felt myself being lifted off the floor. I was staring right into Jake's eyes.

"Wha..." my tongue was all tangled from sleeping.

"I'm carrying you to bed, Darcy. Now stop wiggling. I don't want to drop you." Jake's voice was stern and I knew that I'd better not argue with him.

"I don't want to go to Wendy's room," I protested weakly.

Jake ignored me. "Your mother tells me that I should just ignore this strange behavior of yours, Darcy. She says that I should pretend that it isn't happening and maybe you'll quit trying to sleep in the bathtub or with your head in Bruno's bowl."

His voice sounded both angry and frustrated. I knew he was upset with me, but what could I do about it? How could Jake understand how I felt?

"I have to tell you, Darcy, that I'm having a very hard time ignoring your behavior. I think things are getting out of hand."

"But Wendy doesn't want me in her room! I don't want to sleep there either. Why did I have to give up my room? Why can't I find my own place to sleep—away from Wendy?" I asked Jake seriously. The whole thing made perfect sense to me. Why couldn't he understand?

Jake sighed. "We can talk about this more tomorrow. Tonight you have to sleep in the trundle bed. You have no choice."

No choice. That's what Dad had said about his divorce from Mom. Wendy and I hadn't had a choice in that either. It wasn't fair. Parents just made up their minds about something and they didn't even ask how you felt about it. How did they get away with it? I decided that if I ever had kids, I was going to give them choices—lots of them.

Jake managed to pull out the trundle bed without dropping me or waking Wendy. She was sprawled like a rag doll across the covers. The blanket on the trundle was turned back and it looked as though the bed-in-a-drawer was waiting for me. I wanted to keep fighting but the bed did look inviting. Besides, I was sleepy. I sagged against him and he put me down.

"I was asleep down there, you know," I said, not willing to give up too easily.

Jake pulled the covers up to my chin and tucked them around my shoulders. Then he gave me a long, steady look. "You aren't going to be spending your nights behind the couch, Young Lady."

I stared at him as he turned and left the bedroom. I had a sick feeling in my stomach and tears prickling at the backs of my eyelids.

My dad always called me "Young Lady" when he was angry with me, too.

Six

ON the way to school the next morning, I told Emily what had happened the night before.

"So what are you going to do?" she asked. "There aren't many places left for you to go, are there? Your house just isn't that big."

"I know," I admitted sadly. "I suppose I could sleep in the tent in the backyard. Eric and Ryan just put it up."

"Aren't you afraid you'll get cold? These spring nights can still get chilly," Emily said.

I nodded. It would be cold and scary away from everyone else in the family. If I didn't feel like an outcast before, I sure would then.

Emily saw me shudder. "What's wrong?" she asked.

"Oh, nothing. I was just thinking of the kinds of things that live outside. Worms, snakes, grasshoppers, lizards..." I could just imagine all of those things crawling in at night and sleeping beside me—and on top of me. My throat closed up at the thought and shivers ran up and down my back.

"There's no way you could ever sleep outside," Emily pointed out. "You're too scared of anything that creeps, crawls, or has a tail. And you hate camping. You'd never make it in the jungles of your backyard."

"Gee, thanks," I said. "That doesn't make me feel any better." In fact, it made me feel terrible.

I was so lost in my problems that I hardly realized we were already at school. We went to our lockers and then to math class. At least Emily and I could get away with talking since our math teacher was talking to someone in the hall.

Emily leaned over in her seat and said

quietly, "I've been thinking. There must be someplace in your house that could be your room. It wouldn't have to be big or fancy." Her face got that funny scrunched up look that meant she was thinking very hard. Then she snapped her fingers and looked very pleased with herself. "Hey, I know!" she said. "The basement!"

When I thought of the basement, I thought of the huge, horrible, lumpy green lizard Mom had found down there when we first moved into the house. I'd made a terrible fuss when she'd carried it upstairs on a paper plate and taken it outside.

"No way, Emily," I said. "That place is full of goopy, gross creatures. I'd never sleep down there—not for a second."

"But it's a good idea. There's plenty of room down there and you'd have your own space and—"

"Forget it."

"Are you sure?" Emily asked.

"Yes, never in a million, no, a zillion years would I want to sleep down there."

Emily shrugged. "Then I guess you'll have to sleep with Wendy after all."

The thought of Wendy made me sick. I could see her standing by her bedroom door with her hands on her hips and her favorite nasty look plastered on her face. I mean, who wants to be someplace where she isn't wanted? And the problem wasn't just my room, it was the whole house. Suddenly, I didn't feel very wanted anywhere.

The teacher came back in the room, so Emily and I stopped talking and got to work. It was hard to pay attention to my math problems after the conversation I'd had with Emily. Instead of doing long division on my paper, I started drawing pictures. I drew a picture of our house, then divided it into possible rooms for me. In each room, I put a little stick figure of myself sitting on a tiny bed. The bed didn't seem to fit in anywhere, even in my pictures.

"Darcy?" my teacher called out from the front of the classroom. "Are you having a problem? Perhaps the class could help."

I blushed. "Uh, no. I just figured it out," I said as I scribbled out my drawings and began to work on my long division.

* * * * *

By the time I got home from school, I was pretty depressed. I said good-bye to Emily and walked slowly toward our house. I stared up at my old room from the sidewalk. The curtains were open and I thought about when I used to snuggle up with Frederick on the window seat and watch the sun make rainbows in Finnicula's bowl. Now the window seat was cluttered with stacks of sports magazines and the walls were covered with rock 'n' roll posters.

When I glanced up at the roof, I noticed

something I hadn't really seen before. Under the eves, just below the point of the roof, was a tiny window. Then I remembered what Mom had said when we first moved into the house.

"There's a tiny attic but we probably won't use it," she'd said. "It's too much bother since the only staircase to it is a ladder in the hall closet."

I raced into the house, past my mom, and up the stairs. I flung open the door in the hall closet and there it was—a narrow ladder leading to a trap door in the ceiling. Quickly, I climbed the ladder. I was glad that I wasn't afraid of heights.

The trap door flopped open easily. I pushed my way into the tiny, dusty room. Sun streamed through the window and when I moved, I could see specks of dust floating through the beam of sunlight. The room was small but it was plenty big enough for my sleeping bag, my suitcase, and me! I might even have space to keep Frederick and my other stuffed animals—after I rescued them from Wendy's room. Maybe Mom would get me one of those nets you hang to hold your stuffed animals.

I'd finally found the answer! My heart pounded wildly as I crawled down the ladder. I'd found it! I'd found a place to live!

When Mom wasn't looking my way, I grabbed her bucket of cleaning supplies and a handful of rags, then I headed back upstairs. The little room definitely needed cleaning. And if I hurried, I could have it done before supper. I would have my very own room again. I could hardly wait!

I'd been working for half an hour when Eric's head popped up through the floor of the attic.

"What are you doing, Sprout?"

"Just some cleaning. Go away."

"Hey! What a cool place!" Eric said as he looked around. I didn't know this room was here." He climbed all the way into the room,

then poked his head back through the floor and yelled for Ryan to follow him.

In less than two minutes, my room seemed to have shrunk. Once Eric and Ryan invaded my room, we were pretty packed in.

"All right! This is great!" Ryan said.

"Dirty, though," Eric added. "Maybe it would help if we had a broom."

My head popped up. They were going to help me? I couldn't believe it. Maybe I had been too hard on them—maybe having brothers wouldn't be so bad.

Before I could say anything, the boys disappeared down the ladder. When they returned, they were carrying a broom, a mop, and a bucket of soapy water. They were actually helping me clean my new room!

"I'll sweep," Eric said. "Ryan, you mop the floor. Sprout, how about washing the windows and all the flat places?" He stood up and bumped his head on the sloped ceiling. "Boy, there's not much head space up here," he said.

There's enough for me, I thought.

"Hey, these beams sure look strong," Ryan said. "I'll bet this room could hold lots of good stuff."

I grinned to myself. They actually cared about how my new room would look. Then I remembered. They should care. They're the ones who stole my old room away from me and forced me to live with Wendy.

The boys jumped up and down on the floor like they were testing it. Then they brought a radio upstairs and turned it on full blast. We scrubbed and cleaned the whole place. By the time we went down for dinner, we were all pretty excited about my new room.

I'd planned to tell Mom and Jake about my surprise during dessert, but they had invited Emily's parents over for dessert and coffee. The adults were busy talking about boring things like how tough times were when they were young. Emily and I finally gave up on them and escaped to the attic. I couldn't wait to show her how great my new room was.

We climbed the ladder, and Emily gasped in surprise. "This is great! I love it up here," she said.

"Yeah, and I have to admit, the boys were so nice about helping me clean. They even tested the floor to make sure it was strong enough for me."

"They don't sound like the brothers you complain about all the time," Emily said. "Did they have brain transplants—or did you?"

I shrugged, feeling foolish.

"So, when are you moving in?" Emily asked. "Why don't you wait until after school tomorrow? Then I can help you."

"Okay. I suppose I can stand to sleep in Wendy's room for one more night, as long as I know it'll be my last night there."

We made plans to go straight to my house after school the next day. Emily promised to help me move my things in and set everything up.

After Emily and her family left, I didn't even mind snuggling into the trundle and going to sleep. After all, it was the last night that I'd feel like a cockroach stuffed beneath my big sister's bed.

"Are you ready for the big move?" Emily asked when the last bell rang at school the next day.

"All set," I answered as I gathered my books and put them away. "I can't wait to get going." It was all I'd thought about all day long. I noticed that Mrs. Appletree (the teacher who talked about nomads) had given me a few strange looks when I'd drifted off into wonderful daydreams about my new, Wendy-less life. But she never said anything to me about it.

We ran home so quickly that both Emily and I were puffing by the time we reached our block. We walked more slowly toward my house.

"I hear music," Emily said. "Where do you

think it's coming from?"

"It sounds like your house," I said.

"Or yours." We both stopped to stare at the two houses. I had an icky, sinking feeling in my stomach. I could see people moving around in my attic room.

"That's where the music is coming from!" Emily shouted as she started to run toward my house. "What are people doing in your bedroom?"

We ran into the house, hurried up the stairs, and crawled up the ladder to the attic. When I stuck my head through the opening in the floor, Ryan shouted over the noise of his stereo, "Out, kids!"

"But this is my room!" I yelled back. "You get out!"

"Yours? Since when?" Ryan asked.

"Since I found it! You knew that I found it—you even helped me clean it up!" I argued.

Ryan looked puzzled. "Huh? We didn't clean it up for you. We cleaned it for us."

I must have looked shocked, because Ryan added more gently, "You must've misunderstood us, Sprout."

For the first time, I glanced around the attic. There were free weights and dumbbells everywhere. The walls were lined with weight-lifting posters and charts. It had totally become a boys' room. My ruffled curtains and colorful sleeping bag would never fit in now.

How could I have been so stupid? They hadn't been trying to help me!

"But, but...," I stammered.

"Mom and Dad said it was okay. They never mentioned that you'd asked to use this room," Ryan said.

I felt as though Ryan had just dropped one of his weights on my heart. They'd already asked permission to use the room! But stealing the room from me didn't hit me as hard as when Ryan called *my* mother Mom. She wasn't his mother or Eric's mother! She was *my* mother!

I blinked back a few tears. What gave Jake the right to decide what happened in this house? It was my mother's house. Besides, Mom and Wendy and I were here *first!* I hated them. I hated them all.

Blindly, I turned to go down the ladder, nearly stepping on Emily's fingers. I followed her down the ladder so fast that I nearly knocked her over.

"There's got to be another place for you, Darcy," Emily said. "There's just got to be! We'll just have to find it, that's all."

"You just don't get it, do you?" I snapped back at Emily. "There is no place for me. I have no place to live!" I wanted to scream and cry but I didn't want to do it in front of Emily.

"How about the basement? It's got to be better than you remember it," Emily suggested.

"I already told you it's horrible down there. It's dark and damp and creepy. Water pipes are hanging out of the ceiling and it smells like mud." *And the lizard had been down there,* I thought.

I even avoided going near the basement door if I could help it, especially if it was partially open. I hated that place, even if Mom did have the foundation fixed as soon as she'd found the lizard. Somehow I'd never been able to convince myself that there wasn't a whole nest of slimy creatures down there just waiting to slither up my legs as soon as I stepped on the basement floor.

"But if it were cleaned up...," Emily began.

"It won't work, Emily. Besides, I couldn't, even if I wanted to."

"Why not?"

"Jake is using the basement for his carpentry shop. Mom told him he could have the whole thing."

He gets everything he wants. He and his sons. Mom doesn't care what happens to me anymore. Neither does Dad. And Emily tries, but she just doesn't understand. Nobody does.

Seven

A few days later, Wendy caused another major-league crisis in my life. She managed to save enough of her allowance money to buy a telephone. Can you imagine anything worse than sharing a bedroom with a babbling teenage weirdo?

Wendy's the world's biggest spender. Money stays in her pocket about 10 seconds before she buys some lipstick or eyeliner or a new teen magazine. So it's a miracle she saved any money at all.

From the minute that she had the phone installed, Wendy spent every night in our room talking to anyone within dialing distance. And what's worse, she wanted to be alone while she talked. That meant the bedroom door was always locked—with me on the outside.

"Let me in there, Wendy!" I yelled as I pounded on our bedroom door one night. I could hear her gossiping about Brent Ryder, her latest love interest. The boys were watching football and I was sick of searching for new hangouts where I was safe from Wendy.

"Go away. I'm busy," Wendy yelled through the door.

"You are not! You're only talking to Gretchen on the phone. You've been talking to her for an hour!"

"Go away, Darcy."

"There's not much to say about Brent Ryder except that he's a major dweeb. And he has zits," I yelled.

"He does not!" Wendy said defensively. But it didn't make her mad enough to open the door.

I plopped down in the hallway and waited until Wendy finally came out to use the bathroom—half an hour later. As soon as she walked through the door, I dived into the room, slammed the door shut, and locked it. I had to get my stuff packed. Wendy hollered and pounded on the door and threatened to tell Mom before she finally gave up and left. I was alone at last, but I knew it would be over as soon as Mom heard about the locked door.

I put the clean clothes Mom had laid on the bed into my suitcase. I stuffed Frederick into the side pocket of the bag. He looked squashed in there but I didn't have any choice. If he was going to come with me, he had to suffer a little. I took my time gathering my things together.

I unlocked the door. After I peeked around the door into the hallway to make sure the coast was clear, I picked up my junk and headed toward the stairs. No one heard me slip downstairs. I could hear Wendy in the kitchen complaining to Mom about me. Quietly, I tiptoed out the front door and across the lawn to Emily's house.

I rang the doorbell and Gemma, Emily's little sister, answered it. Gemma was as much a problem for Emily as Wendy was for me. Gemma was five years old and very demanding. Tonight she was wearing pink shorts, a red T-shirt, and mismatched socks. She had strawberry jam all over her face, her hands, her clothes, and now, all over the doorknob. What a mess!

"Hi, Darcy, where are you going?" she asked, looking at my suitcase.

"Just here. Is Emily home?"

"EeeeMmmmEeeee!" Gemma screamed at the top of her lungs without even turning around.

I ground my teeth together in pain. Gemma had nearly broken my eardrums with that screech.

Emily came shooting down the stairs. "Shhhhh! Mom said I should keep you quiet. Oh, hi, Darcy. What are you doing here?"

"Could I stay overnight?" I asked.

"I'm sure Mom won't mind," Emily said happily.

"Forever?"

Emily blinked. "What's going on?"

"I'm running away from home."

"Darcy's running away, Darcy's running away," Gemma squealed, jumping up and down. "Why're you running away? Are your new brothers mean to you? Do they beat you up like on TV when..."

"Gemma, stop it!" Emily yelled. Then Emily pointed her finger toward the family room and Gemma slunk off.

"I can't take it there anymore," I said. "No one will miss me, I'm sure of that. Wendy won't hang up the phone long enough to unlock the bedroom door and let me in. Ryan and Eric spend every free minute lifting their stupid weights in the attic. I'm so mad at all of them."

"What about your mom? What did she do?" Emily asked.

"She doesn't care either. She's so ga-ga over

Jake that she doesn't notice anything that's going on." I made a barfing sound and poked my finger toward the back of my throat. "Blech."

"I'm telling on you," Gemma yelled from the stairwell where she'd hidden. Her beady little eyes stared at us. "I'm telling your mom that you're running away from home, Darcy!"

"Brat," Emily muttered. "Get lost. And don't you dare tell anyone about this. Or you'll be in big trouble."

"Give me a dollar or I'll tell," Gemma said, twisting her curls with her finger.

"A dollar? You're crazy!" Emily said.

"Fifty cents then."

"Okay," Emily said as she fished two quarters out of her jeans' pocket and shoved them into Gemma's hand.

Gemma ran off, happy for the moment.

"She's almost worse than Wendy," I admitted to Emily. "She seems even brattier than she was last year."

"Just wait, you'll be happy Wendy's your sister after a night or two with Gemma," Emily said, making a face.

Emily's mom appeared in the doorway. "Hello, Darcy." She looked at my suitcase and raised an eyebrow.

"She wants to stay here, Mom. Just for a while. Wendy is being a creep and..."

Emily's mom held her hand up like the school patrol guards do. "Let Darcy talk, Emily."

That surprised me so much I hardly knew what to say. No one at my house seemed interested in hearing what I had on my mind. I'd tried talking to Mom about my feelings a couple of times. And though she seemed to really listen to me, she never understood. She just kept saying things would work out. I know she believed that things would get better, but I didn't—not anymore.

"I was just wondering if it would be okay if I stayed here in Emily's room? At least for tonight," I explained.

"Well, I'll have to call your parents first, Darcy," she said, then she disappeared into the other room. Emily and I stared at each other. This was my last chance. What if my mom said I had to come back home? Then what would I do? I paced nervously until her mom came back. She was smiling. "Your mom said it would be all right for you to stay with us for a night or two, Darcy. She said you might feel better."

Sure, she was glad I'd left, I thought as I dragged my suitcase upstairs to Emily's room. Mom had agreed right away to let me stay with Emily. I'll bet Wendy and the boys were dancing around the house to celebrate my leaving.

It wasn't long until I realized that Emily had a problem as big as mine. That problem's name was Gemma. Oh, I'd known Gemma for a long time, but she used to be cute and sweet. I'm not sure when or why she turned into such a brat, but she was definitely a brat.

I'd never realized what it was like to have a whiny little sister who threatened to tattle about everything. I wanted to threaten to tell on her and say mean things back to her but I couldn't, I was a guest. But if she'd been my little sister, I might not have been so nice to her. She was always nosing through my suitcase and once I even found her carrying Frederick under her armpit. So, it came down to a lousy choice—Gemma, or Wendy and the stepmonsters.

The worst thing about Gemma was her sleepwalking. Emily said she did it almost every night. Gemma would wander around the house until she found a cozy bed to sleep in. She especially liked the bed I was sleeping in. It might not have been so bad, but sometimes Gemma wet the bed. Yuk. That was worse than getting my feet wet when I slept in the bathtub!

After only two days, Gemma was getting on my nerves like a bad case of poison ivy.

After dinner the second night, I went outside to get away from her. As I plopped down on a cozy chair, I could see our yard. The tire swing that Jake had put up the first day he moved in hung perfectly still. I thought about the swing and how much fun it had been, especially when Jake had pushed me.

"Hi, Sprout."

The voice startled me. I turned and saw Eric standing near the porch with his hands stuffed in his pockets. He stared at me for a long time. I didn't know what to say to him.

"What are you doing?" he asked. I don't think he knew what to say either.

"Not much," I said quickly. Then I decided to tell him the truth. "Well, really I'm hiding from Gemma," I admitted.

He smiled a little. "She's a real pain, huh?"

"You could say that." I felt like smiling back but I didn't. I wanted Eric to sit down and talk to me. I wanted to know what had been happening at home. I wondered if anyone missed me. I guess I was being silly—I'd only been gone for two days. He'd probably just noticed I was missing.

"When are you coming home?" Eric asked. When I looked at him in surprise, he added, "Uh, well, don't let it go to your head or anything Sprout, but I miss you. It seems funny around the house when you aren't there."

"It does?" My voice cracked.

Eric looked embarrassed, as if he couldn't believe he'd just said that. "Uh, gotta go," he mumbled and disappeared around the corner of the house.

I stayed on the porch for awhile after he left. I had to think. *Why had Eric come over? Did he really come to talk to me? And why had he said he missed me? It didn't make sense!* I was about to go inside when Ryan took a big leap and landed on the porch in front of me. He was carrying a little paper bag.

"Hi. I brought you something," he said.

I was tempted to pinch myself to see if I

was dreaming. First Eric, now Ryan!

"What is it?" I asked.

"Candy bars. Your favorite kind, too." He held them out to me.

"How do you know they're my favorite?" I asked, looking in the bag.

"Wendy told me." That surprised me, too. I didn't realize my sister knew anything about me.

Ryan plopped down in the chair next to mine. "I think Eric and I owe you an apology, Sprout. We didn't think about you when we took over the attic. Eric and I didn't even think that you might be cleaning it up for yourself. We just got so excited about having a place for our weights that we didn't think about anything else." He looked a little sad. "We screwed up, Darcy. I'm sorry."

Suddenly, I realized what he was doing. Mom and Jake probably made him and Eric come over and apologize. They'd probably be grounded if they didn't. And here I was falling for it like an idiot.

"Really? How do I know Mom and Jake didn't put you up to this?" When I looked up at him, I felt stupid that I'd said that. He really looked like he felt bad.

"No, Darce, I meant it," he said.

I believed him this time. Just then Gemma came wandering onto the porch wearing my very best sweatshirt. She was eating a chocolate ice cream bar with one hand and wiping the other on the front of the shirt.

"Gemma!" I yelped. "You're supposed to stay out of my things! Now look what you've done. You've gotten gunk all over my best shirt."

Ryan chuckled.

"What's so funny?" I asked.

"Well, you sound exactly like someone who drives you crazy."

Then I figured out that he meant Wendy. I'd turned into a pint-sized version of Wendy. How scary!

Much to my amazement, Ryan raised his

hand and ruffled my hair. "Come home, Sprout. We're not perfect, but we promise not to wear your clothes or get chocolate all over them!"

It took only a moment to decide. Emily's family wasn't that much better than my own.

"Just a minute," I said. "Let me run upstairs and get my suitcase."

I saw Jake standing at the front door as Ryan and I walked across the yard. He was smiling. He didn't yell or give me a lecture about leaving home without permission. In fact, he even made Wendy get off the phone so that I could have the bedroom to myself for a while.

I put my suitcase next to the trundle and sat down. I had to admit that it felt great to be home.

Eight

"I'm going shopping," Mom announced the next day after school. "Do either of you girls want to come with me?"

"I do," Wendy said. "I have lots of very important shopping to do. There are some things I need to get."

"Like what?" I asked, "Beauty pills? You sure need more of those."

"Very funny." Wendy tossed her hair around like in a shampoo commercial.

Jake chuckled from where he was standing in the doorway. I was glad someone else thought Wendy was as silly as I did.

"What about you, Darcy?" Mom asked as she laid a gentle hand on my cheek. "Do you want to come along?"

"No thanks," I said.

"Eric and Ryan are playing softball," Mom said, "but Jake will be here working in his shop." She gave me a big hug. "If you need anything, just tell Jake, okay?"

I nodded. I wouldn't need anything from Jake. My plan was to call Emily on Wendy's phone as soon as Wendy was out the door. I wanted to fill her in on how things were going. Unfortunately, my plan didn't work.

Emily wasn't home. I tried calling a dozen times, but there was no answer. Bored and lonely, I wandered around the house.

The mailman arrived. I heard him drop letters into the tin mailbox on the side of the house. I opened the door and took the stack of mail inside.

There was a letter for Wendy from a friend who moved last year. Ryan and Eric each got a weight-lifting magazine. There was lots of mail for Jake and Mom. And there was even a letter for me! I tore open the envelope and

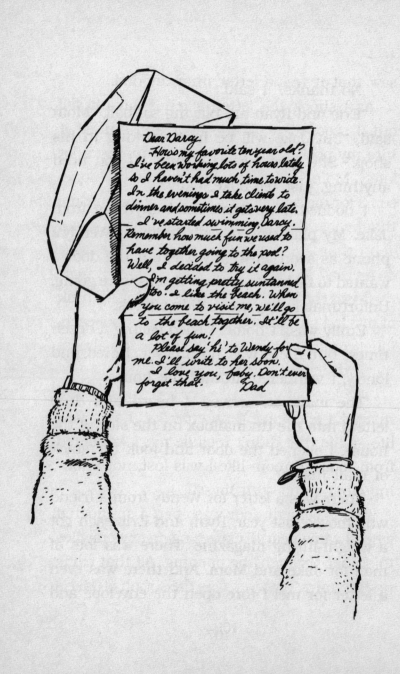

Dear Darcy,

How's my favorite ten year old? I've been working lots of hours lately so I haven't had much time to write. In the evenings I take clients to dinner and sometimes it gets very late.

I've started swimming, Darcy. Remember how much fun we used to have together going to the pool? Well, I decided to try it again. I'm getting pretty suntanned too. I like the beach. When you come to visit me, we'll go to the beach together. It'll be a lot of fun!

Please say 'hi' to Wendy for me. I'll write to her soon.

I love you, baby. Don't ever forget that.

Dad

saw that it was a letter from my dad.

As I shook the letter, a ten-dollar bill fell out. I scooped it off the floor and stuffed it into my pocket. My dad sent me money a lot lately. Mom said it was because he was lonesome for me and looking for a way to show me that he loved me even though he was far away. Ten dollars is nice, but it can't take the place of my dad, especially his big, snuggly hugs.

I read the letter three times. I tried to think of my dad suntanned and playing on a beach. I just couldn't imagine it. In fact, it was almost hard to picture his face in my mind.

The letter didn't make me feel any happier. Instead, I felt worse than ever. Dad had a new life—a life that didn't include me. I wandered from room to room like I was lost, not knowing what to do with myself.

The basement door was open. I shuddered when I came near it, expecting creepy-crawlies to slither through the opening. All that came up the stairs, however, was the sound of Jake's voice as he sang to himself.

I poured myself a glass of milk and ate three cookies, trying to forget how much I missed my dad. As I sat at the table, I realized that it was cozy having Jake downstairs singing like that. My real dad used to sing sometimes. I'd always loved it when he did.

I finished my milk and washed out the glass in the sink. I drifted over to the basement door to hear what song Jake was singing. For a moment, I pushed back the thought of lizards and peeked down the stairs.

Jake had hung new light fixtures. Instead of being dim and spooky, the stairway was bright and friendly. Jake had painted the steps and lined the walls with pale-colored paneling. It looked almost nice down there.

Curiously, I took one step down the stairs and then another. When I was halfway down, I bent to peek at Jake's new workshop.

He was a better carpenter than I'd realized. He'd redone all the walls and painted them

white. He'd even laid a new floor, and I saw a roll of carpeting lying in one corner. Along the wall he'd built a workbench and neatly stored his tools there. The room was bright and cheery and looked very lizard-proof.

"Hi, Darcy!" Jake looked up from his work. "Do you need something?"

I shook my head.

"Come down and see my workshop," he invited. Slowly, I moved toward the bottom of the stairs.

"Are there lizards down here?" I asked. Then I told him about the lizard Mom found and about how horrible it looked skittering around in the middle of that paper plate. I felt myself trembling when I talked about it.

Jake didn't laugh. Instead, he showed me how he'd sealed the basement floor and walls and made very sure that nothing could crawl in and surprise him.

"I don't like lizards either, Darcy. You don't have to worry about that anymore. You may come down here whenever you like," he assured me.

"I wouldn't even have come down today, but it was so boring upstairs," I admitted. I just couldn't tell him I was lonesome.

"Why don't you sit on this stool next to my workbench and talk to me?" he asked. "I was singing to keep myself company."

"I know. I heard you. You have a nice voice." It was easy to compliment Jake on his voice. As we talked, I looked around the basement. Everything looked big and bright and clean.

"Would you like to learn a song I taught Eric and Ryan when they were your age?" Jake asked.

I thought about it for a minute and then nodded. *Why not?* I thought.

We sang every song I knew and dozens that Jake taught me. Soon we were laughing so hard we couldn't sing anymore.

Jake looked at me for a moment and then said, "You're good company, Darcy. I'm glad you came downstairs."

"Me, too," I admitted.

"I thought you'd decided never to talk to me." Jake looked sad as he said the words.

For the first time I realized that Jake was almost handsome. He had nice, thick brown hair and beautiful eyes that could look really happy or sad. I was beginning to see why my mom liked him so much.

I blinked twice and nearly had to hold my jaw from flopping open when I realized what I was thinking. *Was I getting used to Jake? Or was I simply being unfair to my father? Could I like both of them?* I didn't know.

"I'm sorry," I said, feeling very confused.

"I know I'm not your real dad," Jake said. "I'm not trying to replace him. I hope you know that you can like both of us. You don't have to choose between us. I'd never want you to do that. Your dad will always be your dad and a very special part of your life." He smiled sadly. "But I would like to be your friend, Darcy. I feel like I haven't had the chance."

Jake's right. I'd never given him the chance, I thought guiltily. As the afternoon wore on, I learned something more about Jake. I learned that he was a wonderful listener. I found myself talking to him about how it felt to be Wendy's little sister and to be forced to sleep in a trundle bed in her room when I wasn't welcome there. I told him what had happened when I discovered the attic and how I felt Ryan and Eric had taken it away from me. I told him how awful it felt to sleep in a bathtub and to have a baby beagle chew on my hair. Then I told him how much it hurt to live so far away from my real dad.

Jake was quiet as he stood at his workbench. His big hands were busy sanding a piece of wood but I knew he was paying close attention to what I said.

When I heard Mom and Wendy returning from their shopping trip, I was disappointed. My time alone with Jake was over.

Nine

I didn't see much of Jake for the next few days. He spent most of his free time in the basement working on a project. Every night he'd carry lumber and big sheets of wall board down the stairs. He pounded and hammered and sawed until midnight or after. Mom finally asked him to quit working when Wendy and I went to bed so that we could sleep.

Whatever his new project was, it was top secret. He even began to lock the basement door. It seemed funny that at one time I would have been glad to have Jake locked in the basement. Now I missed him when he didn't wander into the family room after supper to watch TV with the rest of us.

Mom's voice interrupted my thoughts.

"Darcy, I need to talk to you," she said.

I looked up from the mystery story I was reading.

"Actually, I need to apologize." Mom looked very serious.

"For what?" I asked.

"For not being sensitive to your needs."

"What do you mean?" I asked.

"Our family has gone through a lot of changes lately," she said. "The divorce, me marrying Jake, moving to a new house . . . suddenly having stepsons has been a big adjustment for me, too. I guess I didn't realize how hard this has been for you."

I hung my head. "I wasn't sure you cared about me anymore."

"Oh, Darcy!"

"Dad left. We moved. You gave my bedroom away. And Wendy thinks I'm a creep. I didn't think there was room for me anymore . . ."

My voice got shaky, like I might cry.

My mother put her hands on my cheeks. "I promise to help you through this, Darcy. It might be hard but we'll make it. Some good things are going to happen soon. You'll see. In fact," her voice got low, as if she were telling a secret, "we'll make good things happen."

Mom put her hand on my head. "Jake likes you very much. And I'll always love you."

If she'd stood there much longer, with that loving look in her eyes, I would have started to bawl like a baby. I was saved by a terrible pounding noise in the basement.

"What was that?" I asked.

Mom smiled. She looked so happy. In fact, I couldn't remember Mom ever being this happy before. I liked it when she was silly and giggly. I guess a lot of it had to do with Jake.

"Jake is working on a very special project," she explained, her eyes twinkling. "He'll show it to us when he's all done."

"It sounds big," I said.

Just then Jake opened the basement door.

"Sorry for all the noise," he said. He surprised me with a big, long wink, as if he and I were sharing a special secret. Mom looked from Jake to me with a pleased expression. I was confused. What kind of secret did Jake and Mom think we were sharing?

Two days later, Jake came into the room I shared with Wendy.

"What are you doing, Darcy?"

"Drawing a picture," I sighed. "I wish I could hang it up in my room."

"Why can't you?" he asked.

"Because Wendy says my junk bothers her," I told him. "The walls are off limits."

"Well, we can deal with that later," Jake said. "For right now, why don't you come downstairs to the basement, Darcy? There's something I'd like to show you."

I was curious. I hadn't been in the basement since that day I'd visited Jake down there. The basement didn't seem so scary to me now that he'd cleaned it up.

"Can I see your new project?" I asked.

"I'd like that," he answered. He held open the door. "You first."

I walked slowly down the stairs, doing a little lizard check as I walked. There were no lizards in sight. Eric and Ryan were standing by Jake's workbench with stupid grins on their faces. Mom and Wendy were there, too, smiling. When I looked around the basement room, I gasped.

"Your workshop! It's smaller!"

"Do you like it?" Jake asked.

"Where did all the room go?" I asked. The long workbench had been cut in half and made to fit around a corner. The stacks of lumber were gone.

"Look behind that door." Jake pointed to a wooden door in the middle of the far wall. Then he led me across the room and everyone else followed us. When we reached the door, he threw it open.

Suddenly, I realized what Jake had done.

He'd divided the basement in half. One half was his workshop. The other half had been made into a bedroom.

"Do you like it?" he asked.

"It's beautiful!" I walked into the room.

It was painted pale yellow, like sunshine. There was a big closet at one end with lots of shelves and drawers. Jake had even made a frame for a king-sized bed. I had a fluttery feeling in my stomach.

"Is this for Eric?" I asked. "Or Ryan?" I had to know.

Jake put his hand on my shoulder. "This is your room, Darcy."

"Mine?" My voice came out in a squeak.

"You had to give up your room because of us. Now I'd like you to have this one."

"I told him to make the bed king-sized so you could flip and flop all you wanted!" Wendy said happily. "You can squirm all night and not fall off this bed."

Then she surprised me by giving me a hug.

"I'm sorry, Darcy. I know I've been really rotten to you lately. I didn't mean to be so nasty about sharing my bedroom with you. I guess I didn't like the way everything was changing any more than you did. Will you give me a chance to try harder?"

"Uh, sure," I stammered. I couldn't believe what I was hearing.

"Oh, and I got you this when I went shopping with Mom. I've been saving for it. I hope you like it," Wendy said, as she gave me a box wrapped in paper that said "For Someone Special." I tore open the paper and in the box was a new phone. My own phone! And it was yellow, to match my new room. I hugged her back.

Then Eric started pulling on my sleeve. "Dad's still working on a new chest of drawers for you so you can finally take your clothes out of the suitcase. What do you think of that, Sprout?"

"And I told Dad he'd better make you a

bookcase," Ryan said. "Every bedroom should have a bookcase."

Mom stepped up and put her arms around me. "I'm making curtains, Darcy. Wendy and the boys picked out the fabric. It's yellow, like the walls. Maybe we could make hanging them a family project some Saturday afternoon. What do you think?"

I nodded, too amazed to speak. My own drawers? No more living out of a suitcase? Curtains? For me?

"Now, Darcy, Wendy and the boys have planned a little party to celebrate your new room." Mom brushed her hands through the air as if to shoo them upstairs. "Come on, kids, let's get out the cake and napkins. I think Darcy is a bit overwhelmed by all this right now. Let's let her enjoy it."

Eric, Ryan, Wendy, and Mom all ran upstairs to get ready for the party. Jake and I were alone together.

He lifted a little square of wood from the

closet shelf. "Hey, I almost forgot. I made this for you, too."

It was a sign that he'd carved especially for me. It said:

DARCY'S ROOM
DO NOT ENTER UNLESS INVITED

Darcy's room. The words sounded good when I said them to myself. What they meant was that finally I had a place where I could be in charge. Finally I had a place where no one could make me leave or be quiet unless I wanted to!

"Darcy," Jake said softly. "Don't you like it?"

"Oh, Jake!" I blurted, "This is the nicest thing that's ever happened to me! The room is beautiful. It's the most perfect room in the whole world, but..."

"But you're still afraid of lizards?" he finished my sentence for me.

I nodded my head unhappily.

"But you're down here now," he pointed out. "And you don't seem afraid."

"That's because you're here!" I pointed out.

A big smile spread across Jake's face when he realized what I'd said.

"Darcy, I'll be in my shop almost every evening working on something or other. That means you won't have to be alone until you get used to being in the basement. Besides, I checked the foundation. This house is very tight now. There won't be any more lizards. There's not a single spot for them to crawl in. And maybe we could talk your mom into letting Bruno stay with you if you're still afraid. He'd chase away any lizards."

I laughed out loud at the thought of Bruno scaring away anything. Jake laughed, too.

Then I got serious and asked, "Are you sure it's safe?"

"You'll have to trust me, Darcy. I know you haven't trusted me before but I'd like you to give it a try."

I looked up at him and nodded. I wanted to trust him. I wanted to trust him very much. "Okay," I said.

He smiled at me. "I'd like to look out for you as though you were my own little girl, Darcy. Would you let me do that?"

I looked around my beautiful new room and realized that Jake was already treating me like I was his own daughter.

I put my hand in his and smiled at him. No, Jake would never be my real dad, but he did care about me. And even though I knew it would take a while to get used to my new family, I wanted to try. I really did.

"Hey, come on up," Eric yelled down to us. "The ice cream's melting."

"We're coming," I called back.

Jake and I walked up the steps to join the party. I felt really good for the first time in a long time. I knew that I'd finally found a place to live.

About the Author

JUDY BAER began her writing career when, at the age of eight, she started publishing her own family newsletter.

Since that time, Judy has published more than 21 books. The idea for *My Mutant Stepbrothers* came from Judy's own experience. In 1985, when Judy needed an office to work in, she decided to use her daughter's bedroom as an office. Her daughter was forced out of her own bedroom and into her sister's bedroom. Neither of her daughters were happy about having to share a room. "Today, my office is in the attic, where I can look at the sky and dream up new ideas for stories," says Judy.

In her spare time, Judy likes to read mysteries, romance, and nonfiction. She also enjoys renovating the old farmhouse where she lives with her husband and daughters, Adrienne and Jennifer, in Cando, North Dakota.